NFL TODAY

THE STORY OF THE HOUSTON TEXANS

NATE FRISCH

CREATIVE EDUCATION

PUBLISHED BY CREATIVE EDUCATION
P.O. BOX 227, MANKATO, MINNESOTA 56002
CREATIVE EDUCATION IS AN IMPRINT OF THE CREATIVE COMPANY
WWW.THECREATIVECOMPANY.US

DESIGN AND PRODUCTION BY BLUE DESIGN
ART DIRECTION BY RITA MARSHALL
PRINTED IN THE UNITED STATES OF AMERICA

PHOTOGRAPHS BY CORBIS (WALTER BIBIKOW/
JAI), GETTY IMAGES (BRIAN BAHR, BILL BAPTIST,
DOUG BENC, STEPHEN DUNN, CHRIS GRAYTHEN,
SAM GREENWOOD, JEFF GROSS, ALLEN KEE/NFL,
BOB LEVEY/NFL, ANDY LYONS, RONALD MARTINEZ,
CHRIS MCGRATH, AL MESSERSCHMIDT, DONALD
MIRALLE, RONALD C. MODRA/SPORTS IMAGERY,
LAYNE MURDOCH, JERALD PINKUS/NFL, JOE
ROBBINS, DAMIAN STROHMEYER, ROB TRINGALI/
SPORTSCHROME, GREG TROTT, JARED WICKERHAM)

LIBRARY OF CONGRESS CATALOGING-IN-PUBLICATION DATA
FRISCH, NATE.
THE STORY OF THE HOUSTON TEXANS / BY NATE FRISCH.
P. CM. — (NFL TODAY)
INCLUDES INDEX.
SUMMARY: THE HISTORY OF THE NATIONAL FOOTBALL LEAGUE'S
HOUSTON TEXANS, SURVEYING THE FRANCHISE'S BIGGEST STARS
AND MOST MEMORABLE MOMENTS FROM ITS INAUGURAL SEASON
IN 2002 TO TODAY.
ISBN 978-1-60818-304-3
1. HOUSTON TEXANS (FOOTBALL TEAM)—HISTORY—JUVENILE
LITERATURE. I. TITLE.

GV956.H69F75 2013
796.332'64097641411—DC23   2012031213

FIRST EDITION
9 8 7 6 5 4 3 2 1

COVER: RUNNING BACK ARIAN FOSTER
PAGE 2: QUARTERBACK DAVID CARR
PAGES 4–5: RUNNING BACK DOMANICK WILLIAMS
PAGE 6: DEFENSIVE END MARIO WILLIAMS

TABLE OF CONTENTS

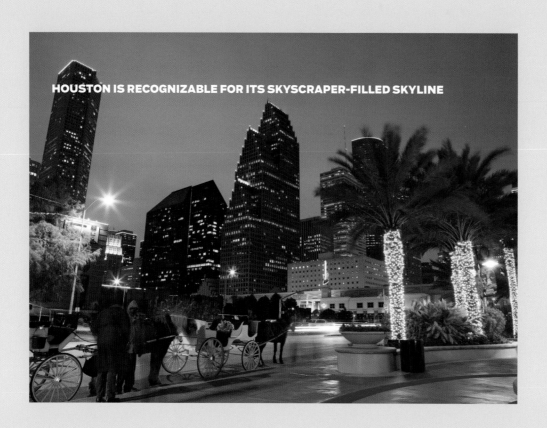

Fighting Texans

Houston, Texas, is a city of humble beginnings and varied identities. Named after Sam Houston, a Texas soldier and politician, the city was initially a distribution center for cotton. The focus changed in the early 20th century when oil was found in the region. The identity of Houston shifted yet again in 1961, when the National Aeronautics and Space Administration (NASA) moved its headquarters to Houston. Today, the fourth-most populous city in the United States maintains a balance of cutting-edge technology and old traditions.

Football in Texas has also gone through many shifts and updates, only to cycle back to the past. Beginning in 1960, the Houston Oilers entertained fans of first the American Football League (AFL) and then the National Football League (NFL). Oilers fans were upset in 1997, however, when the team left Houston (eventually becoming the Tennessee Titans). It was then that businessman Bob McNair began working to

LIKE MOST OF TEXAS, HOUSTON HAS LONG BEEN PASSIONATE ABOUT FOOTBALL

Bob McNair

TEAM OWNER / TEXANS SEASONS: 2002–PRESENT

In 1960, Bob McNair and his wife moved from the East Coast to Houston, Texas, where he developed a high business profile as the founder of Cogen Technologies, one of America's largest privately owned energy companies. A member of the Texas Business Hall of Fame, he was also a horseman, owning a 1,500-acre thoroughbred farm in Kentucky called Stonerside Stables. McNair got into the football business on July 3, 1997, when Houston Oilers owner Bud Adams announced that his team was officially moving to Tennessee. Many fans feared that professional football in Houston was over. And it might have been, had it not been for McNair. Immediately after the announcement, McNair laid out a plan and worked nonstop for two years, campaigning tirelessly until the league finally awarded Houston the NFL's 32nd franchise at a purchase price of a record $700 million. "It really was a feeling of importance to the city and civic pride that was the motivation for me," said McNair. "I thought it was important for the fourth-largest city in the country to have a team. I was in a position, maybe the best position, to make it happen."

HOUSTON SELECTED A BULL AS ITS MASCOT, AS CATTLE ARE PLENTIFUL IN TEXAS

bring a new expansion team to the city. His hard work paid off in October 1999, when NFL owners voted 29–0 to award the league's 32nd franchise to Houston. In the end, a new franchise was established in the longtime NFL city and took on an old AFL name. Decked out in uniforms of blue, red, and white, the Houston Texans were born.

To begin building his new team, McNair hired Charley Casserly as the team's general manager, who in turn hired Dom Capers as head coach. Capers had a reputation as a master at building defenses. He also had a history of success in building teams from scratch. In just two seasons, he had taken the expansion Carolina Panthers all the way to an appearance in the National Football Conference (NFC) Championship Game in 1996. "I know the type of work that's involved in building an expansion team," said Capers. "You have to work hard, have a plan, and not take shortcuts."

The Texans began building their player roster in an expansion draft held in February 2002. Houston was able to grab several quality performers left unprotected by other NFL teams, such as five-time Pro Bowl offensive tackle Tony Boselli of the Jacksonville Jaguars, tough defensive tackles Gary Walker and Seth Payne, cornerbacks Aaron Glenn and Marcus Coleman, and linebacker Jamie Sharper. Casserly and Capers made sure to choose players who were still in their prime and showed strong leadership skills. "We know that there will be some tough times ahead," said Sharper, a starter on the Baltimore Ravens' Super Bowl championship team in 2000. "We have to be strong for the young guys."

fter the expansion draft, the Texans had only a few weeks to prepare for the NFL Draft. Fortunately, the team knew exactly who it wanted to choose with the number-one overall pick: quarterback David Carr from Fresno State University. The 6-foot-3 and 230-pound passer had all the physical tools to be a great NFL quarterback—a cannon of an arm, quick feet, and great field vision. After selecting Carr, the Texans showed their commitment by signing him to a seven-year contract.

Houston plucked some other promising offensive players from the 2002 NFL Draft as well. Speedy wide receiver Jabar Gaffney from the University of Florida gave Carr a quality passing target, while powerful linemen Chester Pitts and Fred Weary were selected to protect the young quarterback.

The Texans also found some solid players in the free-agent market, signing big-play receiver Corey Bradford from the Green Bay Packers, center Steve McKinney from the Indianapolis Colts, and linebackers Kailee Wong and Jay Foreman from the Minnesota Vikings and Buffalo Bills respectively. With the team finally assembled, it was time for the dream that was the Houston Texans to become a reality.

The Texans' first opponent in Reliant Stadium, their home field, was the five-time Super Bowl champion Dallas Cowboys—often referred to as "America's Team." For the Cowboys, the game was an opportunity

An Improbable Victory

On September 8, 2002, the Texans' very first regular-season opponent was a high-profile one: the Dallas Cowboys, winners of five Super Bowls. The 69,000 fans inside Reliant Stadium didn't have to wait long for something to cheer about, as, on the third play from scrimmage, Houston quarterback David Carr zipped a 19-yard touchdown pass to tight end Billy Miller. Houston made it 10–0 on a 42-yard field goal by kicker Kris Brown before Dallas tied the game 10–10, and the momentum seemed to shift. But the Texans weren't done yet. Carr hit Corey Bradford for a 65-yard touchdown strike early in the fourth quarter, giving Houston a 17–10 lead, and the Texans' defense did the rest. Tackle Seth Payne sacked Cowboys quarterback Quincy Carter in the end zone for a safety, and the Texans held on for an improbable 19–10 victory as the Houston crowd went crazy. "It was kind of unbelievable," Miller said. "We had history against us. I think just us and the coaches and probably our wives were the only ones who thought we could win."

DAVID CARR CELEBRATES VICTORY AFTER THE TEXANS' INAUGURAL GAME

THE FIRST TEXANS STRUGGLED WITH PASS BLOCKING, GIVING CARR LITTLE PROTECTION

to squash the young Texans and put them in their place. For the Texans, the game was a chance to make clear that Texas was not exclusively Cowboys country anymore.

The Texans jumped out to an early 10–0 lead with a 19-yard touchdown pass from Carr to tight end Billy Miller and a field goal by kicker Kris Brown. Houston's defense kept Dallas's offense corralled as the Texans secured a 19–10 victory. In doing so, Houston became the first NFL expansion team since the 1961 Minnesota Vikings to win its opening game. "I don't know what the rest of the season holds," said Houston running back James Allen, "but this win will be remembered for a long, long time."

Aaron Glenn

CORNERBACK / TEXANS SEASONS: 2002–04 / HEIGHT: 5-FOOT-9 / WEIGHT: 185 POUNDS

Aaron Glenn grew up in Humble, Texas, and attended Nimitz High School, where he lettered in football, basketball, and track. The multitalented Glenn decided to pursue football and went to college at nearby Texas A&M University, where he became a two-time All-American as a defensive back and punt returner. He spent eight strong seasons as a cornerback for the New York Jets, becoming one of the NFL's best cover men, despite his short stature. In 2002, the Texans brought Glenn back to his home state by nabbing him in the league's expansion draft. And he didn't disappoint. Glenn had a career year in 2002, earning his third career trip to the Pro Bowl. His best game that season came against the Pittsburgh Steelers, when he dominated by picking off two Steelers passes and returning them for touchdowns. "He's got great quickness, great change of direction, and almost unmatched physical ability in covering people," said former Jets coach Pete Carroll. "He can score touchdowns from the defensive side of the field. He's a very special athlete."

Battle Red Day

Every season since 2003, the Houston Texans have designated one or two home games as "Battle Red Day." On these days, the players wear special red jerseys instead of their usual blue uniforms to help drum up extra support for high-profile matchups. Fans, cheerleaders, the Bull Pen Pep Band, and even Toro the mascot dress in red to help get the team fired up. And the tactic seems to work. On November 2, 2003, Houston took on the powerful Carolina Panthers at Reliant Stadium dressed in Battle Red for the first time. The outlook did not appear promising for the Texans, since quarterback David Carr was out with an injury and backup quarterback Tony Banks was in his place. The game was close, but in the fourth quarter, with Houston trailing 10–7, Banks led the team down the field and finished off the drive with a 20-yard pass to tight end Billy Miller, who made a spectacular one-handed grab in the end zone to secure a 14–10 Houston win. All told, from 2003 through 2012, the Texans went 9–4 on Battle Red Days.

RELIANT STADIUM BECOMES ESPECIALLY RAUCOUS ON BATTLE RED DAYS

Welcome to the NFL

Following the Texans' grand entrance into the NFL, the rest of their inaugural season held just three more victories. Two were tightly contested, with Houston defeating the Jacksonville Jaguars and New York Giants by scores of 21–19 and 16–14. The other was a surprising blowout win on the road over the playoff-bound Pittsburgh Steelers. Aaron Glenn led the way to the 24–6 victory with two long interception returns for touchdowns.

Although team success was limited, Glenn's 5 interceptions and Gary Walker's 6.5 quarterback sacks earned them each a trip to the Pro Bowl. Carr played admirably, especially considering the young quarterback was sacked 76 times, a new single-season NFL record. "People wondered if David had the guts to take the pressure of being a starter in the NFL," said Coach Capers. "He got knocked around a lot this year, but he never flinched. He's the real deal."

Andre Johnson

WIDE RECEIVER / TEXANS SEASONS: 2003–PRESENT / HEIGHT: 6-FOOT-3 / WEIGHT: 222 POUNDS

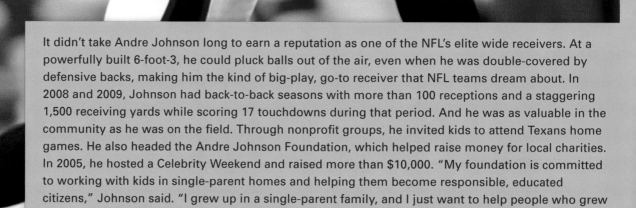

It didn't take Andre Johnson long to earn a reputation as one of the NFL's elite wide receivers. At a powerfully built 6-foot-3, he could pluck balls out of the air, even when he was double-covered by defensive backs, making him the kind of big-play, go-to receiver that NFL teams dream about. In 2008 and 2009, Johnson had back-to-back seasons with more than 100 receptions and a staggering 1,500 receiving yards while scoring 17 touchdowns during that period. And he was as valuable in the community as he was on the field. Through nonprofit groups, he invited kids to attend Texans home games. He also headed the Andre Johnson Foundation, which helped raise money for local charities. In 2005, he hosted a Celebrity Weekend and raised more than $10,000. "My foundation is committed to working with kids in single-parent homes and helping them become responsible, educated citizens," Johnson said. "I grew up in a single-parent family, and I just want to help people who grew up in the same situation that I did."

"He's the real deal."

DOM CAPERS ON DAVID CARR

Before the 2003 season, Houston concentrated on providing Carr more pass protection and a better supporting cast. The Texans began looking in the free-agent market, signing massive veteran tackle Zach Wiegert. Then, in the 2003 NFL Draft, Houston selected big receiver Andre Johnson, speedy linebacker Antwan Peek, and stout halfback Domanick Williams. Fans were most excited about the 6-foot-3 and 222-pound Johnson, who possessed a rare combination of speed and strength. His addition gave Carr a big target who had the potential to score every time he touched the ball.

The 2003 Texans got off to another quick start, upsetting the heavily favored Miami Dolphins 21–20 on the road in the first game and becoming the first NFL expansion team to win its first two regular-season openers. Another highlight came three weeks later in Reliant Stadium, when, on the game's final play, Carr made a one-yard touchdown dive over a pile of players to beat the Jaguars 24–20. Houston's improved offense was encouraging, but linemen injuries crumbled the foundation of the Texans' defense. Although Houston finished its second season just 5–11, several players put forth impressive showings, including rookies Williams (1,031 rushing yards) and Johnson (66 receptions) and veteran cornerback Marcus Coleman (7 interceptions).

Houston was determined to keep moving up the AFC South standings in 2004, but it wouldn't taste victory until Week 3 against the Kansas City Chiefs. Down 21–14 in the fourth quarter, the Texans converted on 4th-down-and-1 with a punt fake to keep the drive alive. Houston made the most of the opportunity as Johnson gained 37 yards on a sensational juggling catch. Then Carr found Gaffney in the

Inside the Bull Pen

Located in the north end zone of Reliant Stadium is a special bleacher section called the Bull Pen. It is there that hardcore Houston fans gather to cheer on their Texans. Forty-five minutes before the game, fans led by the Bull Pen Pep Band march into the stadium, onto the field, and then into their seats. Obnoxious behavior is usually not tolerated in the rest of the stadium, but fans in the Bull Pen are encouraged to stand throughout the game and interact with opponents via such actions as turning their backs when the opposing team scores a touchdown. The Bull Pen Pep Band—a 45-member musical group that performs at all home games—is another unique element. Before games, the band can be seen marching through the parking lot among tailgaters. During the game, they play songs between quarters and when the Texans score. Between the fans and the band, Reliant Stadium can be a noisy place for opposing teams. "This place gets pretty loud when everyone's into the game," Houston receiver Andre Johnson said. "It rates up there as one of the loudest places in the NFL."

VOCAL FAN PARTICIPATION—AND COSTUMES—ARE STANDARD IN THE BULL PEN

MARCUS COLEMAN GAVE AND RECEIVED SOME BIG HITS IN 11 NFL SEASONS

end zone to tie the game. After Houston's defense forced a Kansas City punt, the Texans drove into field goal range. With only seconds remaining, Brown booted a 49-yard game-winner.

In the next game, running back Jonathan Wells stepped in for an injured Williams and rushed for 105 yards, helping Houston defeat the Oakland Raiders. The victory marked the first back-to-back wins in franchise history. "Our team showed what we are capable of doing," said Gary Walker. "We set a standard for the rest of the season." After seven games, Houston was a solid 4–3 with real hope of making the postseason.

That hope faded, however, as Houston lost five of its next eight games. Going into the last game of the season at 7–8, all the Texans had to do was overcome the struggling, 3–12 Cleveland Browns to achieve their first non-losing season. But Carr had difficulty moving the Texans' offense. Houston fans booed as he threw for only 114 yards, and the Texans limped to a 22–14 defeat. "We need to be slapped in the face," said Miller. "It was despicable. It was disgraceful. It was one of those learning experiences."

Despite the crushing loss, Houston had posted its best season to date, going 7–9. Johnson set a team record with 1,142 receiving yards and became the first Texans offensive player to earn a trip to the Pro Bowl. Williams also had a season to remember, carrying the ball for 13 touchdowns.

GARY WALKER WAS VALUED FOR HIS ABILITY TO STUFF RUNNING ATTACKS

Unfortunately, the Texans' 2004 improvement was followed by a 2005 setback. Houston opened the season with six straight losses, finally entering the win column in Week 8 when Carr threw some long bombs and connected with rookie wide receiver Jerome Mathis for a 34-yard touchdown strike. Mathis also added a 63-yard kick return late in the fourth quarter that set up the game-winning field goal. The fast-rising rookie continued to shine for the rest of the season, rolling up 1,542 total yards and 2 touchdowns on kick returns. Despite his heroics, the Texans won only one more game and ended the season with a 2–14 mark.

To shake up the struggling franchise, McNair fired Coach Capers the day after the 2005 season ended. During his four seasons in Houston, Capers had built a combined record of just 18–46. "I understand the job as the head football coach is to win games," Capers said. "But when you put your heart and soul into something and it doesn't work the way you want it or anticipate it to, it's disappointing."

Styling Stadiums

Houston has a rich history as a trendsetter in stadium technology. In 1965, the city introduced the Astrodome, the world's first domed stadium, as a home for both football's Houston Oilers and baseball's Houston Astros. In 2002, Houston built Reliant Stadium at a cost of $352 million. Reliant Stadium was the first NFL arena to have a retractable roof; the roof was made of translucent, Teflon-coated fiberglass and could open and close in just 10 minutes. Reliant Stadium housed two 360-foot-wide scoreboards, one above each end zone. The stadium also featured a 10,000-square-foot weight room (the largest in the league) that included a 3-lane pool. In addition to its state-of-the-art features, Reliant quickly became known as a tough place to play, as cheering fans sat closer than usual to the edge of the field, making it difficult for opposing teams to hear. Houston players such as safety Eric Brown appreciated both the stadium's lush playing surface and its home-crowd volume. "The grass is easy on your body," he said, "and the fans are right on top of you."

RELIANT STADIUM HAS HOSTED RODEOS, SOCCER MATCHES, AND OTHER EVENTS

GARY KUBIAK WAS AN NFL BACKUP QUARTERBACK BEFORE HE WAS A COACH

Kubiak Takes Command

To replace Capers, the Texans hired former Denver Broncos offensive coordinator Gary Kubiak. In his 11 years as a coordinator, Kubiak had helped guide the Broncos to back-to-back Super Bowls and had sent 28 different offensive players to the Pro Bowl. "The number-one thing you need to do to get things going is to have aspirations and to have a standard," said Kubiak. "My dream is to see this city win a championship someday."

In the 2006 NFL Draft, Coach Kubiak and the Texans picked up smart linebacker DeMeco Ryans in the second round and tight end Owen Daniels in the fourth. But the Texans' most promising—and controversial—draft choice was the first overall pick, defensive end Mario Williams out of North Carolina State University.

The 2006 Draft featured some exceptional players, including flashy running back Reggie Bush and big quarterback Vince Young, a Houston native who had just led the

MARIO WILLIAMS WAS THE MOST CONTROVERSIAL DRAFT CHOICE IN TEAM HISTORY

DeMeco Ryans

LINEBACKER / TEXANS SEASONS: 2006–11 / HEIGHT: 6-FOOT-1 / WEIGHT: 239 POUNDS

When DeMeco Ryans came out of the University of Alabama and entered the 2006 NFL Draft at "only" 6-foot-1 and 239 pounds, many scouts thought he was too small to become a star middle linebacker. But instead of seeing his supposed physical limitations, the Texans saw his playmaking ability, great instincts, and upbeat attitude. "He's got some special leadership qualities about him," said linebackers coach Johnny Holland. "He's got the [ability to get] people around him to play better." From day one, the easygoing Ryans proved that he was up to the challenge of leading an NFL defense. With a rarely seen combination of determination, confidence, and intelligence, he led the league with 126 solo tackles and earned the NFL Defensive Rookie of the Year award. In one game against the Oakland Raiders, Ryans forced one fumble, recovered another, sacked the quarterback, and intercepted a pass, becoming the first player in Texans history to do all four in one game. When Ryans left Houston following the 2011 season, he did so as the club's all-time leader in tackles.

ANDRE DAVIS BOOSTED HOUSTON IN THE LATE 2000s WITH HIS KICK-RETURN SPEED

University of Texas to a national championship. Fans and football experts across the country assumed Houston would select one of the two offensive stars. So when the Texans drafted and signed Williams instead, it put the sports world in a tizzy. Houston fans who were at Reliant Stadium for a public draft party booed the choice. "It's a decision that took us a lot of time to make," said general manager Charley Casserly, "but at the end of the day, we felt this was the best player for our football team."

In Kubiak's coaching debut against the Philadelphia Eagles, the game started well, as the Texans drove down the field on their first possession and scored a touchdown. But the offense fizzled thereafter, and Houston lost 24–10. The team lost the next two games as well before Kubiak claimed his first coaching victory in Week 4 when the Texans beat the Dolphins 17–15.

Houston won just 3 games out of the next 10, and as Carr struggled with fumbles and interceptions, fans began booing, having lost patience with the fifth-year quarterback. But Kubiak, a former quarterback himself, knew that the whole team needed improvement. "The quarterback gets a lot of the credit and he gets a lot of the blame, but as a football team, we have to look in the mirror, because there are plenty of mistakes in a lot of areas," the coach said.

As other Texans players picked up the slack, Houston won its final two games of the season. Against Indianapolis, veteran running back Ron Dayne, a new addition, rushed for 153 yards and 2 touchdowns, and Brown booted a last-second, 48-yard field goal to help Houston defeat the high-powered Colts for the first time in 10 tries. Rookie running back Chris Taylor then stepped up with 99 rushing yards and a touchdown in Houston's final game of the season, a victory over the Browns.

At the conclusion of the 6–10 season, the Texans made a major change by

ROOKIE CHRIS TAYLOR SURPRISED FANS WITH A BIG RUSHING GAME IN 2006

Mario Williams

DEFENSIVE END / TEXANS SEASONS: 2006–11 / HEIGHT: 6-FOOT-7 / WEIGHT: 291 POUNDS

When Mario Williams was selected with the top overall pick in the 2006 NFL Draft, some Houston fans booed, and others cried. NFL experts had been saying for months that the struggling franchise had lucked out in the draft by getting their choice of two surefire stars—fleet-footed running back Reggie Bush or 6-foot-5 quarterback Vince Young—and now Houston had passed on both. But those fans had not seen in Williams what the Texans' scouts had. The defensive end from North Carolina State was huge, fast, and agile, and he had a knack for wreaking havoc in offensive backfields. "He can change a game the way he rushes the passer and the problems he presents for an offensive team," said Texans coach Gary Kubiak. In 2006, Williams fought through a foot injury to start all 16 games—a show of determination that earned him the respect of his teammates. Then, in 2007, as Bush struggled in New Orleans and Young endured his own ups and downs in Tennessee, Williams silenced any remaining critics by notching 14 sacks and 59 tackles to emerge as a bona fide star.

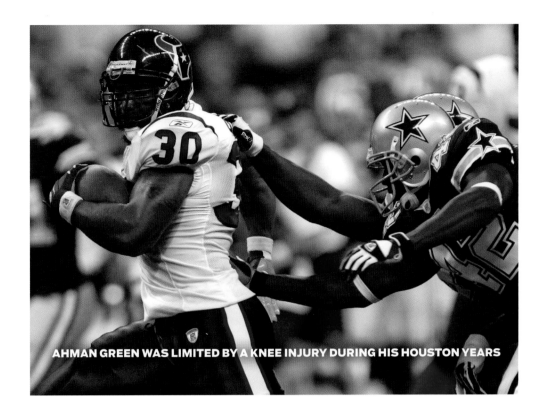
AHMAN GREEN WAS LIMITED BY A KNEE INJURY DURING HIS HOUSTON YEARS

releasing Carr and trading with the Atlanta Falcons for 25-year-old quarterback Matt Schaub, who had backed up star Michael Vick the previous 3 seasons. "We wanted a player who's ready to go into his prime, and that's what this young man is," Kubiak said. "This guy is ready for his opportunity to run a football team." Before the start of the 2007 campaign, the Texans also signed former Green Bay Packers star running back Ahman Green and drafted defensive lineman Amobi Okoye.

In the first game of the 2007 season, the Texans whipped the Kansas City Chiefs 20–3. Mario Williams had the best game of his young career, making two sacks and returning a Chiefs fumble for a Texans touchdown. Offensively, Schaub and Johnson hooked up for a 77-yard touchdown pass. The next week, Houston defeated the Carolina Panthers 34–21 on the road, overcoming an early 14-point deficit. For the first time in team history, Houston was 2–0.

The Texans hit a rough patch in the following weeks, however, losing five of the next six games. But they wouldn't give up. Even with injuries sidelining key players such as Johnson, Green, and Schaub, Houston continued to battle, finishing the season 8–8. "It's huge," defensive end N. D. Kalu said. "You've got to start somewhere, and this is just another stepping stone. We won 6 last year and 8 this year, and hopefully we'll win 11 next year."

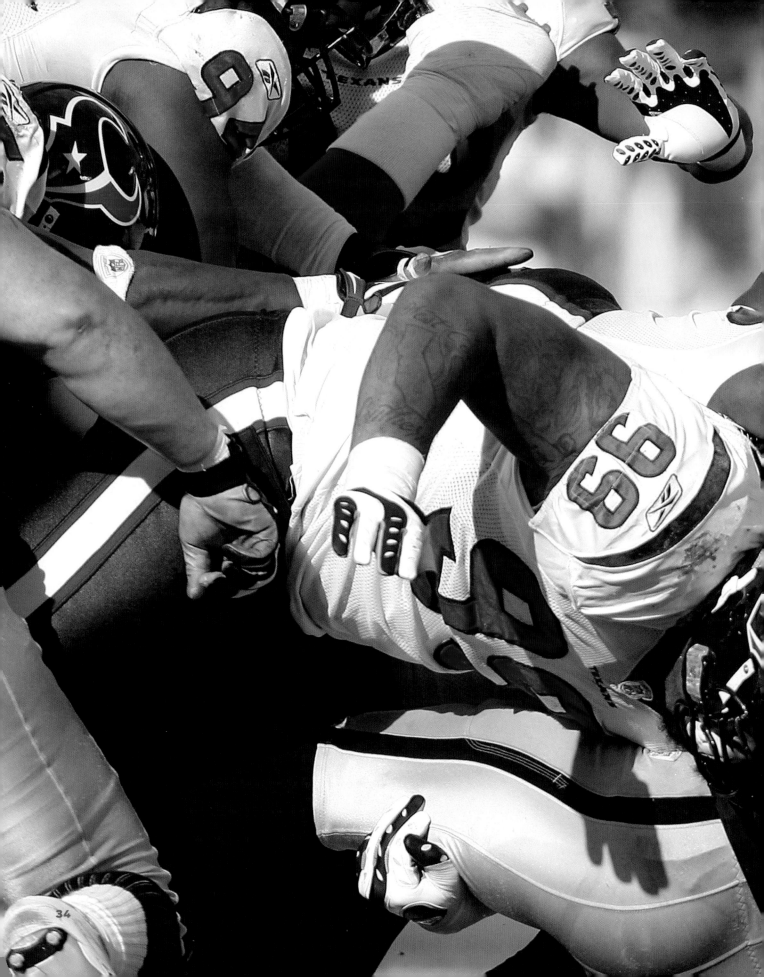

BY 2007, THE TEXANS WERE STARTING TO SHOW THEIR HORNS, GOING AN EVEN 8–8

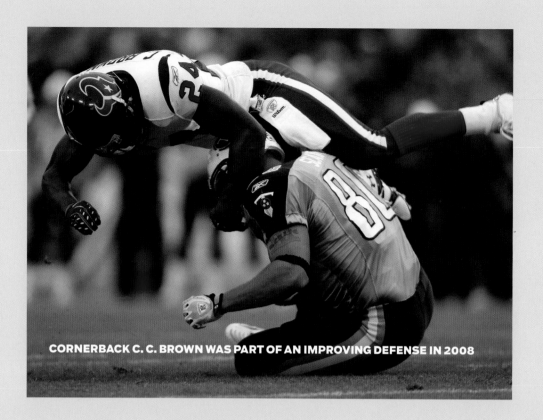

CORNERBACK C. C. BROWN WAS PART OF AN IMPROVING DEFENSE IN 2008

By Air or by Ground

alu and the rest of the Texans hoped that the return of a healthy Schaub and Johnson and the drafting of running back Steve Slaton would give Houston the offensive star power to become a contender in 2008. However, the season began with 4 straight defeats, including a late-game collapse in which the Texans blew a 17-point lead in the last few minutes of a contest versus the Colts.

Remarkably, the Texans bounced back from that devastating loss and proved a tough opponent the remainder of the season. Slaton exploded onto the NFL scene by dashing for 1,282 yards and 9 touchdowns. He also caught 50 passes, while wideout Kevin Walter hauled in 60 and tight end Owen Daniels tallied 70 receptions. This trio complemented Johnson's amazing 115-reception season to give Houston a formidable passing attack.

This developing aerial assault was put on full display in a cold, late-season game in Green Bay. Houston set a team record with 549 offensive yards, including a 75-yard

STEVE SLATON'S GREATEST NFL SEASON WAS HIS FIRST, AS HE TOPPED 1,000 YARDS

Pick Your Poison

In 2009, Texans quarterback Matt Schaub led the NFL in passing yards. In 2010, the guy lining up behind him in the backfield was Arian Foster, who led the NFL in rushing yards that season. Although the two players shared a common goal of winning games by whatever means necessary, there seemed to be an unofficial weekly competition as to which player could put up the most mind-boggling numbers. The gauntlet seemed to be thrown down in the first two weeks of the 2010 season when Foster set a franchise single-game rushing record with 231 yards, and the very next game, Schaub shattered Houston's single-game passing record with 497 yards. Although they did not reach such extremes the rest of the season, Foster did have rushing performances of 180, 143, 133, and 127 yards, while Schaub's next bests were 393-, 337-, 325-, and 314-yard showings. "One week they run for 300 yards, and the next week they throw for 500," Dallas Cowboys coach Wade Phillips said of the Texans' offense. "If you back off …, they can just tear you up in the running game. If you come after them, they can throw it."

MATT SHAUB AND ARIAN FOSTER GAVE HOUSTON A ONE-TWO PUNCH IN 2009

drive that took less than 2 minutes and set up a last-second, game-winning field goal as the Texans bested the Packers 24–21. And although the Texans ultimately fell short of the playoffs with another 8–8 record, the excitement level in Houston was rising. "We're getting used to winning around here, and that's what we've been looking for," said Ryans.

In 2009, Schaub would remain healthy all season, and playing every week seemed to agree with him, as he led the NFL in passing yards with 4,770. He also completed an impressive 68 percent of his pass attempts and threw 29 touchdown strikes. The Texans' defense, meanwhile, got a boost in 2009 with the addition of versatile rookie linebacker Brian Cushing, who tallied 133 tackles, 4 interceptions, and 4 sacks in his first pro season.

"He can change a game the way he rushes."

The improvements on both sides of the ball helped Houston win its last four games to finish with the franchise's first winning record, but at 9–7, the Texans just missed the playoffs. This near miss was made even more painful with the remembrance that, of Houston's seven losses, five of them were by a margin of a touchdown or less. "We only had one game where we really didn't have a great opportunity to win the game," McNair said after the season. "And we've never been in that position before, so I think [Coach Kubiak has] done a good job of managing the club, and he's done it dealing with some adversity that could have pushed us in the other direction."

If the 2009 Texans had an Achilles heel, it was their running game. So, in the 2010 NFL Draft, after selecting cornerback Kareem Jackson in the first round, the Texans used a second-round pick to acquire Auburn University halfback Ben Tate. Going into the 2010 season, Tate was projected to be the club's featured back, but those plans were derailed when a preseason injury sidelined him for the year. Second-year halfback Arian Foster stepped into the starting role and shocked everyone with a huge Week 1 performance in which he rushed for more than 200 yards and keyed an upset victory over the Colts. Foster would prove this was no fluke by going on to lead the NFL in rushing yards in 2010.

Meanwhile, Schaub was still orchestrating a lethal passing attack, and by season's end, Houston's offense had rolled up the third-highest yardage total in the NFL. Unfortunately, while the offense

The Bengals' Biggest Fans

As the 2009 NFL season wound to a close, the Texans had a shot at earning a playoff bid for the first time in franchise history. In their season finale, the Texans came out of a hard-fought battle against the New England Patriots with a 34–27 victory. Following the game, the Texans became Cincinnati fans. This was due to the fact that the Bengals would be playing the New York Jets, who were competing with Houston for the last AFC Wild Card slot in the postseason. Unfortunately, the Bengals—who'd already clinched a playoff berth of their own—came out unmotivated and, after falling behind early, pulled most of their starters to rest them for the postseason. As Cincinnati was crushed 37–0, so too were Houston's playoff hopes. "I'm disappointed with the way Cincinnati played," Texans owner Bob McNair said. "As it turned out, they just left their game at home." Houston received some consolation two years later. The Texans earned their own way into the 2011 postseason and, in their first ever playoff game, faced the team they had once rooted for. The Texans embarrassed the Bengals, 31–10.

THE TEXANS IN ACTION AGAINST THE BENGALS DURING THEIR 2011 PLAYOFF CLASH

HOUSTON'S DEFENSE SURGED IN 2011, BECOMING ONE OF THE NFL'S STINGIEST

TEXANS DEFENSIVE STANDOUTS MARIO WILLIAMS (LEFT) AND AMOBI OKOYE

was firing on all cylinders, Cushing, Ryans, and Williams all missed time because of injuries, and the weakened Texans defense ranked 29th in points allowed. Houston finished a disappointing 6–10.

In a reversal of roles, it was Foster who was dinged up heading into the 2011 season, and Tate got a chance to show his stuff, amassing 301 rushing yards in 3 games before a healthy Foster could return to action. The duo would combine to rush for 2,166 yards, which helped to compensate for injuries to both Schaub and Johnson. While the Texans' overall offensive production dropped slightly, the defense showed marked improvement. Houston's tenacious pass rush was led by burly young linebacker Connor Barwin, who recorded 11.5 sacks and swatted down 7 passes. The Texans' grittier style of play led to a 10–6 record and the franchise's first playoff berth.

In Houston's postseason matchup against Cincinnati, the Bengals appeared to take control early, marching down the field and scoring a touchdown on their opening drive. The Texans' defense would stiffen the remainder of the contest, however, intercepting three passes and allowing just three more points all game. On offense, rookie quarterback T. J. Yates and Johnson connected on a 40-yard touchdown strike, and Foster chewed up 153 rushing yards for 2 touchdowns as Houston ran away with a 31–10 victory. "I'm just very proud of all the guys, and the job they did," Kubiak said after the win. "Hopefully, there are some more [victories] to come."

The next week, Houston clashed with Baltimore. Unfortunately, it was the Ravens' defense that came up with three interceptions this go-round, and the Texans were unable to overcome an early deficit,

Arian Foster

RUNNING BACK / TEXANS SEASONS: 2009—PRESENT / HEIGHT: 6-FOOT-1 / WEIGHT: 229 POUNDS

As running back Arian Foster finished his college career at the University of Tennessee, part of one NFL scouting report read, "[Foster] lacks the explosiveness to consistently make defenders miss in tight quarters and is not the power runner his size would indicate. Inconsistent." Foster went undrafted in 2009 but was later signed by the Houston Texans. He would rush for just 257 yards his rookie season and was slated to serve as a backup in 2010. But when Houston's prospective starting running back suffered a season-ending ankle injury in the preseason, Foster moved up the depth chart. And after the 2010 season opener, Foster shed his "backup" label for good. In that game, he proved he had both explosiveness and power, maneuvering around and plowing through defenders for 231 yards and 3 touchdowns in a stunning upset over the heavily favored Indianapolis Colts. Foster kept his foot on the gas all season, finishing with 1,616 rushing yards and 16 touchdowns. He also caught 66 passes for another 604 yards and 2 touchdowns, cementing his reputation as one of the most versatile—and consistent—threats in the NFL.

BRIAN CUSHING (LEFT) WAS A PUNISHING TACKLER FROM HIS MIDDLE LINEBACKER SPOT

SCHAUB'S OFFENSIVE DIRECTION LED HOUSTON TO THE PLAYOFFS IN 2012

falling 13–20. Although disappointed, Houston had made great strides, despite missing key players for much of the campaign. Having finally broken the playoff ice, the Texans were confident of more success to come.

For most of the 2012 season, that confidence was fully justified. Johnson had a career-best season, pulling in 112 passes and racking up 1,598 yards. Second-year defensive end J. J. Watt had a monster year, becoming the first player ever to record 16.5 sacks and 15 tipped passes in a single season. He was named AFC Defensive Player of the Year and was a unanimous choice for first team All-Pro. Schaub and Foster also had outstanding seasons as Houston won 11 of its first 12 games. Fans began to sense there would be an opportunity to enjoy home-field advantage in the postseason. Even though the Texans lost three of their final regular-season games, they managed to capture their second consecutive division title. Houston's defense was dominant in a 19–13 win over Cincinnati in the Wild Card playoffs, but the Texans had no answer for Patriots quarterback Tom Brady the following week, giving up a 41–28 contest in the next round.

In a city and a state that has long appreciated football, older Houstonians still value the days of the Oilers. But this progressive city and its residents have proved willing and eager to embrace the developing Texans franchise and its rising stars. In return, the up-and-coming team with the Lone Star bull on its helmets is eager to soon give its committed fans an NFL championship to cheer about … and to build a legacy the city of Houston can one day look back on with pride.